D0688396

Cornell Elem. School Library
920 Talbot Ave.
Albany, CA 94706

DISCARDED

CORNELL SCHOOL LIBRARY

THE Prince OF Ireland AND THE Three Magic Stallions

retold by

BRYCE MILLIGAN

illustrated by

PRESTON McDANIELS

Holiday House / New York

For Mary, the love of my life
and the best storyteller I know
B. M.

Text copyright © 2003 by Bryce Milligan
Illustrations copyright © 2003 by Preston McDaniels
All Rights Reserved
Printed in the United States of America
The text typeface is Colmcille.
The artwork was created with Russian watercolor
with graphite.
www.holidayhouse.com
First Edition

Library of Congress Cataloging-in-Publication Data
Milligan, Bryce, 1953–
The Prince of Ireland and the Three Magic Stallions /
retold by Bryce Milligan; illustrated by Preston McDaniels.—1st ed.
p. cm.
Summary: In this retelling of an Irish folktale,
the prince of Ireland's stepmother curses him
to stay no longer than two nights anywhere until he brings her
a giant's horses from the western edge of the world.
ISBN 0-8234-1573-2
[1. Fairy tales. 2. Folklore—Ireland.]
1. McDaniels, Preston, ill. 11. Title.
PZ8.M632 Pr 2001
398.2'09417'02—dc20   00-032042

T 421263

There once was a king in Ireland who had a young queen. They had one son, and all was well and naught was ill. But one day the queen fell sick, and God called her away, leaving the king of Ireland with only his one son and a great sorrow.

Three years and a day passed, and finally the king took a second wife. Then all was well and naught was ill, for after a year and a day she bore him two sons, as like as two lambs.

Now it's many adventures the king's eldest son had. Every day the prince went out hunting and harrying the counties of Ireland, and there wasn't a deer in the land so swift that the prince couldn't catch it, and there wasn't a fox so clever that he couldn't track it down. The king took great delight in the doings of his eldest son, for the prince would hold the throne after him.

Thus it went year upon year, well and not ill, until the boys came of an age to hunt with their elder brother. Then what was well seemed even better, for the three princes became fast friends.

But the young queen watched her husband closely, and at last an evil thought came to her: "The king does not love my sons so much as his eldest. They will never amount to more than the uncles of princelings. I must clear the way to the throne for my own sons."

So one day, the queen called for the king's eldest son.

The prince put aside his hounds and horses, and sat with the queen, chatting and playing at cards. The queen won the first hand, and the prince won the second. "There's a fine thing." He laughed. "We're both satisfied, having won a hand each."

"I will be satisfied," she said, suddenly letting her anger show, "for I lay upon you a *geis*, to perform or die, that you are not to sleep two nights under the same roof nor eat two meals from the same fire until you have brought me the three magic stallions that the young giant Sean O'Donal keeps at the edge of the western world."

Shocked though he was, the prince knew the rules of the deadly game. "Then I lay a *geis* upon you, to perform or die, that you must stand before the high cross by the hermit's chapel with a sheaf of oats in the one hand and a needle in the other and eat nothing but what comes from the sheaf of oats and passes through the eye of the needle until I return."

"My lord, have mercy," she cried. "It's starved I'll be, or frozen, or both. Release me from your *geis* and I will release you from mine."

"I cannot," he said. "No *geis* was ever laid upon a prince of Ireland that he did not perform or die in the trying. Thus I am bound, and thus are you."

So the queen went out to the high cross. There she stood with a sheaf of oats in the one hand and a needle in the other, and it's a miserable creature she was.

But that's the way of the world—some things go well and others ill. The two half brothers of the eldest prince of Ireland came to him sick with sorrow, saying, "We will go where you go and do what you do, for it's a wicked trick our mother has played upon you for our sakes."

So the three of them mounted their horses and rode into the west—passing like wind over the plains until they came to a black oak wood.

Beyond the wood they could hear the crashing of the seas upon the shore of the edge of the western world itself.

Then the prince of Ireland said to his brothers, "I've come upon this place before in my ramblings. Hide yourselves away and you'll see a sight worth a song in our father's high hall."

Across the meadow came four great gangly girls, each carrying upon her back a bound rick of hay. Giants they were, and none too comely with their wild hair like dry winter branches and their fingernails like rusty twisted daggers.

"We're well beyond the hearing of our brother, Sean O'Donal," said one, "and I'm in the mind for a bit of a *ceili*." The others agreed, and one pulled out a tin whistle and began to blow. Now she played right badly; and with the wheezing of the whistle and the great pounding of their feet and the timeless flailing of their arms, it was all the young men could do to keep from hooting with laughter.

But the eldest prince of Ireland said, "Shisht—did you not hear that these are the sisters of the giant Sean O'Donal? Let us hide inside these ricks of hay and see where it is this stroke of luck will take us."

At last the giant sisters stopped their dancing to pick up their bundles. "Aargh! This is heavy," complained one after another. But the last sister picked up the rick of hay that had no man inside. "You're just tuckered from the dancing." She laughed, and off they walked. Now all was well and naught was ill, for soon they came to the great horse barn of Sean O'Donal and there they pitched the hay upon the floor and locked the door behind them.

So it was that the princes found themselves right in front of the three magic stallions. They waited for night, until they could hear the snoring of the giants.

Then the prince of Ireland said to his brothers, "Get up and take hold of the white stallion yonder." Carefully, the boys crept up to the stall. But the stallion let out such a neigh that Sean O'Donal jumped out of his sleep and cried to his old washer-woman, "Washerwoman, go and see who it is that would try to steal my horses."

Well, the washerwoman went to the barn and rattled the lock and peered between the slats. But she returned, saying, "Master, the door of the barn is well locked and your stallions are all there."

When the snoring rose again, the eldest prince of Ireland said, "Great stallion, you're the finest horse in all the world. Your coat is like to snow upon the high hills and your eyes are clear gems. I am the eldest son of the king of Ireland, and I am under a *geis* of strong magic to take you and these other noble beasts before our queen."

Much to their surprise, the great white stallion spoke. "I am honored that such as you would attempt this deed. But I too am under a powerful spell, that no living man may lead me from this place unless Sean O'Donal himself gives me to that man as a free gift."

"If that's the way of it, then I must do what I must do," said the prince, sighing. He reached up and patted the stallion's neck, then stood back and put his fingers in his ears. The stallion let out such a neigh that it shook the hills themselves.

At that, Sean O'Donal jumped out of his sleep and cracked his stony skull upon the roof beam. As mad as only a young giant can be, he rushed out to the barn. With six fingers on each hand, and five toes on the one foot and four on the other, and with blood running down from his head and with fire in his eyes, he was a fearsome sight to see.

Now it wasn't well at all, in fact it was very ill indeed, for Sean O'Donal thrust open the doors only to find three defiant princes, swords in hand. "It's well caught you are," said Sean O'Donal. "What can you say for yourselves?"

Then the eldest son of the king of Ireland spoke up, saying, "Sean O'Donal, I'm the prince of Ireland, and these be my brothers. I'm under a *geis* to bring these three fine horses before the queen of Ireland herself, and neither you nor wind nor water will keep me from that task."

"Ho haaaar!" bellowed the giant. "You're a bold little coney, my prince." Then laughing as the swords broke upon his stony hide, he tied each brother up to the roof beam, for though he was but a dozen years old, he was full twice as tall as a grown man, with all the deviltry of youth. Under the dangling toes of the three, Sean O'Donal built a fire.

"Prince of Ireland," he asked, "was it ever in a worse fix than you find yourself now?"

"Aye, indeed I was," he answered, "and a hundred times worse at that."

"Would you be for telling me the story of such a bad fix?" asked Sean O'Donal, for there was nothing he liked better than a good story.

"That I will if you'll be after letting me and my brothers sit beside that fire rather than roast over it," said he.

So that was done, and the giant growled, "Let's have the telling of your tale, and know that your lives depend upon your telling."

Sean O'Donal and his four gangly sisters sat to listen. Outside the door, the old washerwoman peered in. All was as well as it could be, so the eldest son of the king of Ireland took courage, and this is the story he told.

Once upon a day when I first began my ramblings, not far at all from this very place, I came upon a great stone hall, and in this hall I found a woman keening as if her heart would break. "Whatever is it that causes you such sorrow?" I asked.

Said she, "Oh, I am prisoner to a giant, and last night he brought me this babe asleep in the wheelbarrow there. And he has given me orders that I am to cook him a stew using the child's heart and its big right toe. And if I fail to do it, he will kill me as well."

"As to that," said I, "we shall see. 'Twould be a pity to kill a babe for a giant's hunger."

"A pity indeed," said she, "and a crime against nature itself, for the babe is of giant's blood as well."

I looked in the barrow and, indeed, there was a babe the size of a yearling colt. So I said, "Cut off the child's toe if you must, but I will cut the heart from a ram I saw outside, and you shall make the stew with that." So she made a potion to make the child sleep, and she returned to cook the gruesome stew.

Then we heard the giant coming. He was old and he was mean and his tread was like thunder. But the old woman greeted him and served up the stew. Well, no sooner had he eaten than he laid himself down to sleep. I took hold of a pitchfork and heated it red-hot in the fire. Then I thrust it into his eyes, blinding him. In an instant he was up and cursing.

I had just slipped out the door when he called to me, "Wait! I must reward with a golden ring any mortal who escapes me." And he threw out a ring the size of a bracelet. I picked it up and slipped it onto my arm.

"It'll bring the wearer luck," he said. "Put it on."

"It's on my arm, it is," I bragged.

Then he bellowed out, "Squeeze, Ring, squeeze," and the ring squeezed tight upon my arm so that I could not get it off.

Then he yelled, "Ring, Ring, where are you?" And the ring answered in a high clear voice, "Here am I." And with that the giant leaped upon the spot where I had been standing.

Well, there we went, he hollering and jumping, I jumping and running, until we came to the edge of Loch Conn. I grabbed up a stone and I smashed away at that ring until it broke in half. Then I flung the pieces far out over the waters. Well, at that very moment the giant cried out, "Ring, Ring, where are you?" And the ring answered just before it hit the water, "Here am I!"

I suppose that old giant could not swim, for he made a great leap of it and came down in a deep part of the lake. He sank into the waters screaming, and that was the last I ever saw of him.

"Now was that not as bad a plight," said the prince of Ireland to Sean O'Donal, "as for you to put a fire beneath my toes and hang me from a roof beam?"

"That was a grand story indeed," said Sean.

Now the giant's old washerwoman spoke up. "Sean O'Donal," she said, "you must be letting these princes go free, for this story is the very truth itself. And if you doubt it, look at your own right foot where your big toe should be. It was that very toe that the old giant ate, and I am the very woman and this is the very man who saved your life that day."

Well, after that, the giant couldn't give enough honor to the eldest prince of Ireland.

"Anything that is mine you may have," said Sean O'Donal. "Take my sisters, my horses, my gold."

And the eldest son of the king of Ireland said, "May I have the horses?"

"Indeed you may, " said Sean.

So all was well and naught was ill. As soon as the princes were mounted, Sean O'Donal shouted, "Away like wind upon the sea, take these three where they would be!" And before you could snap your fingers three times, they were riding up before the gates of their father, the king, for that was the magic that was in those stallions—besides, that is, the ability of the great white stallion to carry on polite conversation with an Irish prince.

At once they rode into the yard of the hermit's chapel, and there, standing before the high cross, the queen stood shivering with cold and hunger and all. Then the eldest son of the king of Ireland called out to her, "I bring to you the three magic stallions of Sean O'Donal, and your two sons as well. I release you from the *geis*."

Then all was well and naught was ill. The queen's fear of the king's love for his eldest son had melted away, for standing before the high cross in the wild wind with her people gazing on had taught the queen humility. Her sons were given large estates, side by side, and everyone was well pleased.

As for the eldest prince of Ireland, well, his adventures were hardly at an end. But those are tales for other tellings, each one well worth the waiting for.

AUTHOR'S NOTE

Old stories are like large snowballs rolling down a hill. They grow, gathering details with each telling. Sometimes they break apart into two or three stories; sometimes they hold together and become a cycle of related tales, or even an epic. Sometimes the added details were invented on the spot by a storyteller, in Ireland called a *shanachie* [shan i KEY], and some were brought from other stories from other lands.

"The Prince of Ireland and the Three Magic Stallions" is one of those very old stories that can be found in hundreds of different versions. The story has been classified by Aarne-Thompson as Type 953; in the Grimm Brothers classification system, it is Type 191a. The closest version to the one given here is known as "The Black Thief." Major motifs found in this story also occur in many other well-known tales. For example, we find that the three magic stallions are almost identical to the three vials of magic water found in "The Well at the World's End." The wicked stepmother who tries to get the king's first son to risk his life by accomplishing an impossible task occurs in many stories as well.

The story retold here is similar to a version I heard as a child, but I've included details from other versions. I have not attempted to reconstruct the earliest version; rather I have tried to bring some of the wild hares into line.

Readers familiar with Irish stories will recognize the word *geis* [gaysh]. A *geis* is a kind of magic spell, or curse, under which a person must do what he or she is ordered or suffer a severe magical punishment, up to and including death. But a *geis* was rarely laid on another person without the favor being returned. Thus they occur in pairs. The most common form of this *geis* is to sleep no more than one night in a place and to eat no more than one meal at the same table. Another Irish word in this story is *ceili* [kay LEE]. It means a "dancing party."

Folktales are meant to be told. It is fun to dig about in old books in old libraries, reading folktales from around the world, but it is sheer delight to hear one while sitting by a fire on a windy winter's night. "The Prince of Ireland and the Three Magic Stallions" is written down after the style in which an Irish *shanachie* would tell it—with a lilt and a bit of brogue. So find someone to read it out loud.

Sláinte!

Bryce Milligan